beautiful, violent things

madeline anthes

word west press | brooklyn, new york

isbn: 978-1-7369477-4-6

published by word west in brooklyn, ny

first us edition 2021

printed in the usa

www.wordwest.co

cover photo: jordi vaquero

cover & interior design: word west

To J and G: my beginning, middle, and end

table of contents

Tell Me I'm Different

When we meet you will tell me you're tired of the same old thing. You will look me up and down and see what you like.

I will nod and tell you *I know, baby*. I will show you all the ways that I'm different.

I like football and beer and steak.

I am sarcastic and cynical and charming and funny.

I am sexy but I don't seem to realize it. I am strong and gentle and feisty and weak all the ways you want me to be.

You will smile and buy me a drink — a Manhattan or old fashioned — something manly and sweet. You will tell me I look sexy as I wrap my tongue around the straw and pull it into my mouth. You will watch as I sip slowly. Swallow with precision.

You will tell me you wonder if my mouth tastes sweet too.

As sweet as you want. Cherry cola. Sweet tea. So sweet your lips will pull back and you'll smile hard until you grimace.

You will put your arm around my waist to show everyone that this one is taken. *This one.* Me. I'm taken.

I will whisper in your ear and lean against you. *Take me somewhere.* You will feel so needed.

You will ask where I want to go but you already know.

\#

You will run your hands down the granite countertops in my kitchen.

I love to cook. You will smile because you want someone to cook for you like your mother did. Dinner on the table at 6:00, snacks during the game.

You will lick your lips at the thought of me in an apron, poised over the stove. Hair in a bun, sweat forming at the base of my neck.

You will take the drink I give you and watch my hips as I lead you down the hallway.

\#

I will pull you onto the bed. You want me to take control.

You're mine now, I will tell you, and you will nod and nod.

I will tell you things to make your chest rise and fall for me. I will tell you how different you are.

You smell so good.

You are so chiseled.

You are so funny and built and not fragile in any way.

You are so strong and I feel so safe with you.

You will be just like every man. Cologne soaked and whiskey drunk. Clumsy fingers and dull eyes.

I could just eat you up.

\#

While you sleep I will find your cracks and dig my fingers in. I know where to look. It doesn't take much pressure to pop you open, core you from the inside. Leave you hollow.

What did you expect?

The other girls would have let you leave them, hollow them. They would have let you remain whole while they tear out their own insides bit by bit.

I am just what you wanted, I will tell you once I've pulled your sheets up over your shell of a frame. I will tuck you in so gently. This will hurt in the morning.

Tell me again how you want something different.

Punk Rock Princess

1.

I want to be the kind of girl with big teeth and smaller lips. The kind who can smile with my mouth closed or open, not afraid her gums might show too much.

I am careful to curl my lip over my gums now; I don't want to smile too big.

I want to have long nails, painted and hard. The kind that can tap on a counter, or rest delicately in a man's palm. I watched movies with princesses reaching their hands out to a prince, fingers extended, delicate and precise. They had dancer fingers — long, graceful — that landed with a gentle caress in his outstretched hand.

I practiced with my own hands, placing my fingertips into the palm of my other hand, as though I was asking myself to dance.

2.

In high school I listened to boys who sang in high voices, their lyrics crying about heartbreak and loneliness. They pined for their emo girls. These girls strung them along and crushed them, and the songs made my heart pound with ache.

I was jealous of these girls. I pictured them in my mind, envisioning girls I'd never be. They wore skinny jeans and tank tops, eyes lined in thick black kohl, their hair glossy and straight. They pouted in the crowd, the singer pointing every lyric at her like a dart. They rolled their eyes, and bit their lips, beautiful in their dismissal.

In the hallways I walked past the boys with their arms draped around willowy girls and heard myself willing them to look. *Look at me, notice me. Pick me this time.*

I wanted to be a girl from the songs. That girl could break down a boy and change him. That girl inspired and devastated. But I was a ghost with a beating heart and a voice that echoed empty down the hall.

3.

I spent half my life begging to be seen, and the other half trying to disappear.

They see me when I'm trying to blend in, be alone in a crowd. At the gym with my headphones on, checking out at a grocery store, loading bags into my car. I can hear the tune in my head, a rhythm I know too well: *Walk past me. Look past me. Don't look at me. Please. Please.*

But they don't listen.

They force me to look, to put my hands over my face, to smile. I want to turn it off, to tune them out, but once you're seen you can never be invisible again.

4.

I sing when I'm alone. I let my voice crack and fall. I let it echo off my ceiling, off my steering wheel.

I want the burns. I want to be seen and not seen and feel invisible and beautiful.

I think of the emo girls. I think of studded belts, their swaying bodies, their tear-streaked cheeks. I used to think they enjoyed the lyrics written for them. But maybe they were looking for a way out. Maybe all they wanted was to blend in the crowd, to listen to a song about heartache, to be unburdened and invisible. Maybe all they wanted was to dance by themselves.

Birth and hunger and other primal needs

They take Ella's baby daughter away before she can hold her. Around Ella, there is a frenzy of glistening silver tools, bedsheets, and scrubs. The room smells like her own body — blood and sweat and a strange mixture of rust and antiseptic — but she can't smell that now. She is tracking the small bundle being carried around the room, trying to read the doctors' faces as their eyes scrunch in shock and concern. A moment ago Ella had been the most important person in the room. All eyes were on her, holding her hands, monitoring her heart, helping her breathe. Now she is all but forgotten as the doctors and nurses flock to her daughter. Her husband, who has been so stoic and strong through the whole ordeal — from her egg retrieval through her final push — turns away from her, from them both, and looks out the window.

Ella needs her daughter with an urgency so strong it is like a contraction. She lets her mouth open into a scream and cries out for her girl. It is a guttural, piercing cry. A primal cry. Finally, finally they hand her over, and Ella's breast swells with awe at the sight of her. There she is, her perfect baby, covered in glistening red feathers, flexing her wings at the sight of her mother. Her beak opening, closing, opening. There, there, Ella says, while the room looks away. *Let's find you something to eat.*

When Your Ex-Lover Walks on the Moon

I was in love and you were married and that was fine until it wasn't anymore. You chose her and I learned to think about other things. You took up so much space.

I watched you land on the moon. I ached as you combed your fingers through moondust. I know what your hands can do.

I hope you think of me as you look at Earth. I hope you search for me in the clouds of green and blue. I hope you feel far away. I hope you're thinking of my hands. You know what they can do. You know what they've done.

Mary, Wendy, Rosalita

My mother is Mary, a vision.

This is the first song she teaches me — a song of womanhood, of being unattainable. A song of burning pasts and longing.

We sing it with the windows down, our hair whipping into our open mouths. We sing about guitars and roses. A sundress fluttering around bare ankles and chipped porch paint. A breeze pushing a woman to dance carefree.

I am a child and I want to dance. I want a long sundress and a long car ride and I want to sing for my mother forever.

My mother is Mary, a song for the lonely.

#

My mother is Wendy, a woman behind a closed door.

Now I am older. I sing of revved up motorcycles and long legs. I imagine jean shorts and summer heat, a sweet fever sweat that would take me one day. I am not old enough to know lust, but I can feel it coming like the tingle on my skin when a cold breeze heralds a storm.

I want to know why everyone is running. I want someone to love me for my sadness. I want to die in a kiss that never ends, the screams of cars circling us on a dead end street.

My mother is too far away to hear me but I keep singing for her. I want to sing loud enough for the world to hear me. I want someone to sing back. I want to know if I'll ever be wild, too.

My mother is Wendy, a broken hero.

#

My mother is Rosalita, a temptress.

I see her dance recklessly, closed eyes and open palms. He is singing directly to her, charging her. She is filled with pulses and sound, movements and lights. She is electric.

For the first time, I see her as a woman. A woman beyond me, outside of me; the woman she was before me.

I want to wash myself in that vision of her dancing and let it purify me.

My mother cannot hear me amongst the hundreds of voices singing, but she knows my voice is out there. I will always sing for her.

My mother is Rosalita; she is dynamite.

\#

My mother is a woman, an image of myself.

I let the waves of sound move me, let them take me places and make me want.

I am Mary, letting the wind push me to dance, to sweep my feet along chipped paint and ignore the splinters.

I am Wendy, chrome sleek and velvet fast: breathing heat and running wild.

I am Rosalita, waiting to be liberated. Soft and sweet and explosive. Secretive and burning and dangerous. Stone cold desire.

My mother is a woman, a universe.

Call if You Don't Feel Better in Two Weeks

Breathe in that baby smell

I smell lavender body wash. I am curled on the floor of my bathtub, and my sister is showing me how to relieve my over-swollen breasts. I am too weak and too sick to stand. Though the cascading water is hot I am shivering. She shows me how to massage away the pain, but I am too cold and too weak. She covers me with a towel and helps me out of the tub.

I smell hospital. Antiseptic and lunchmeat. My son is in the back of my room, my husband bouncing him to soothe him as we wait for another doctor. We stare at the closed door, the barrier between my newborn and the many invisible threats to his underdeveloped body. When a security guard jokes about how bad it is to bring a newborn to the ER, we want to hurt him.

I smell ginger—the cookies I can stomach when I can't eat anything else. I smell my husband's deodorant as he smooths my hair when I'm too sick to get out of bed.

I don't smell my baby. I don't want to.

#Dontblink

I become obsessed with time. I want it to speed up. Whisk me away to a future place when things are better. I don't know what "better" means. I just know it's different.

I think about how quickly time passed before the baby, and hope it goes as fast after. Our vacation to Seattle was two months ago, and those two months felt like one distended moment. How can I make the next two months go just as fast?

They say to soak it in now because I'll blink and it'll be over.

I blink and blink and blink and time still feels sticky and slow.

I held you instead

I read about leaving the laundry for later. I read to let the dishes pile up. I read that I should let other people help me. I should enjoy this fleeting time with my baby.

I haven't been in my kitchen in a week. I orbit from the bed to the couch. I want to do the dishes.

I want to fold my laundry and wipe off my counter. I want to see something clean, stacked, orderly, complete.

I savor the feeling of clean clothes against my skin.

I cannot hold my baby.

Mom and baby are happy and healthy.
I scroll through my phone and see beaming women holding their babies. They are secure in their hospital beds. I want to warn them that it changes once they get home. But it doesn't seem to change for them. Why did it change for me?

Settling into a new normal they say. They joke about finally getting a shower. They use hashtags like #newmomlife and #needcoffee to make light of it all.

I want to make light of it all, but it all feels so heavy.

I am not happy and I am not healthy.

I miss those newborn noises.
I hear him through walls. I hear each grunt, each cry, each sniffle. Each noise sets sparks across my skin and makes my heart race. I cannot sleep when he sleeps, as they tell me to do. He is too loud. I am too frantic.

When my mother holds him downstairs, I listen through the crackly silence to hear him cry.

I stay in the shower too long and let the water crash on my ears. It's the only place I can't hear him.

This. Right. Here. This is everything.

I ask people to keep telling me it gets better. It gets better, right? It gets better, right? Tell me it gets better?

I don't want this to be all that's left for me. Please tell me that there's more.

And just like that...
I post pictures of my baby. He is smiling and it feels like a salve. People tell me he always looks happy.

I don't post about the night we held him as he screamed, when he wouldn't latch and we knew he was starving. I don't post about my husband feeding him with a syringe or the feelings of defeat and fear that I couldn't care for him.

I can't figure out how to share my child with the world. I want to, but the internet strips away complexity. Everything is black or white. Everything is amazing or terrible.

I want to be many, many things, but I am reduced to just a mother.

What We Bury

I buried my girl on the top of the hill overlooking the lake. I carved out the earth and placed her tiny body at the base of our oak tree, the roots cradling her in their webbed fingers.

I can see the spot from my kitchen window; I wonder if I'll ever stop looking for her.

\#

We weren't ready for a baby. I was shaking as I showed him the pink stick, and we cried together in our double bed, watching our future dissolve into a foggy unknown. We were going to travel. We wanted to be alone.

I wished and wished this baby away.

\#

I started spending more time at the tree. Before work, while I shucked corn for dinner, after a long bath.

My girl had needed so much and filled every moment; I didn't know how to fill the endless stretching seconds now that she was gone. How had I spent them before her? Would they ever feel full again?

Each beat of each day is punctuated by her absence.

#

I didn't love her for the first few months she was inside me, but when she kicked me something changed. She was a fighter like me.

I imagined the bits of her she'd get from us. My ability to make small talk. Her father's ability to wriggle out of a difficult conversation.

After he fell asleep each night, I'd whisper to my belly, asking her questions about who she would become.

#

He left two days after we found her, still and helpless in her crib. She was six months old, and we'd already realized that she was the last thread holding us together.

He said he couldn't look at me. She'd had my eyes. He said he'd never be able to look at me and not see her.

We'd spoken so many nevers together. We'd never stop loving each other. We'd never let anything come between us. I'd meant these words when I said them, but I understood why he left. Our nevers hadn't considered something like this. This kind of sadness would never touch us.

\#

I found myself talking to her after she was in the ground. I asked her questions. *Your eyes were still milky gray — what color would they become?* The tree started answering. I imagined the different colors her eyes could have turned — nut brown like mine, or frosty blue like her dad's. I pictured her big eyes blinking at me. A simple motion, a reflex, that I'd never see again. As I was turning this pain over in my mind, an acorn dropped from the tree and landed next to my hand. I picked it up, and felt a warmth spread from my fingertips and into my chest. Brown eyes like mine.

A day later I imagined her as a twelve-year-old, long-legged with downy hair spread over her calves, free from the embarrassment and awkwardness that would consume her soon. Unburdened, brazen-hearted. *Would you love the outdoors as I hope you would?* As I asked the tree, a flower fell from the branches and landed at my feet. It was a beautiful red tulip that had no business in an oak tree. I knew the tree was answering *yes*.

\#

The answers got stranger as time went on. A ribbon

fell when I asked if she'd be a tomboy, a sure no. A blue feather fell when I asked what her favorite color would be.

When I asked what her career would be, a stethoscope fell from the sky with a thump. When I asked her what she'd do for fun, a Jane Austen novel toppled down and splayed open at my feet.

I didn't question it. Why would I when I was getting the answers I craved? I kept these answered prayers in a shoebox under my bed. I counted them each night, placing them next to each other on my bedspread. Together, they painted a picture of the girl she would have become, the woman she'd grow into.

But there were countless holes to fill; I needed to know everything.

\#

I asked harder questions. *What would her pet peeves be? A cigarette fell. Who would she fall in love with?* Down came dogtags on a silver chain.

But one day I asked a repeat question. I wasn't thinking and asked what her favorite season would be. The first time a golden leaf had fallen from the sky, despite it being springtime. This time, a flower fell.

I panicked and asked it another repeat: *Would she have children of her own?* The first time two pennies had fallen. This time a nickel.

A cavern opened up within me. I had been filling it with these soft answers, these possibilities, but what if the tree had been lying?

What if there could never be answers because she was never meant to have a future?

\#

I buried the shoebox on the other side of the oak tree.

I still look out the window, but I can't bring myself to sit near it again. She's there, willing me to come to her, sit with her, dream with her. But I can't let myself imagine anymore.

She was here once, and now she is not.

I watch the wind blow through the oak tree's leaves and listen in the silence for the sound of her cries.

The Ghost that Haunts my House

The ghost that haunts my house comes home drunk on Thursday nights. Every Friday morning she sits at the edge of my bed and tells me she'll never do it again. But every Thursday night she paints her lips in my mirror and curls her hair around my barrel iron and tells me not to worry.

I try to hold her hair back as she wretches into my toilet, but the tendrils slide like storm clouds through my fingers.

The ghost that haunts my house tries on my clothes and leaves them in piles on the floor. She picks them up when I tell her to, but she complains the whole time. She leaves soda cans and cigarette butts on my kitchen counter.

I tell her to clean up after herself, that I can't have her here if she's just going to make a mess. She smiles a toothy smile that turns my stomach.

\#

The ghost that haunts my house taunts me. She laughs as I prep my week's meals on Sunday afternoons. She sneers as I iron my sheath dresses and blazers for work and calls me frumpy. She changes the channel to teen dramas as I'm settling down to watch Netflix documentaries on Friday nights.

Are you as bored as I am? she asks as I do crossword puzzles in bed.

I tell her it's not about boredom. It's about growing. It's about the process. It's about wanting to climb and earn and be better. Her eyes glaze over in a pearly stare and she tilts her head. She calls it a waste.

\#

I wonder how much more I can stand her. She takes up no space and yet fills every room. Her voice echoes through my bathroom and down my hallway, her high-heeled footsteps clicking through the attic all night.

I am red-eyed and frantically tired from caring for her, picking up after her, talking to her when she cries.

I tell her to leave. That I'm sorry. I have to focus, be serious. I need to sleep again.

I'll leave when you want me to, she says. But you don't want me to go.

She starts to float toward my front door to test me, and I reach for her hollow wrist to pull her back.

No, I say. *No. I'm not ready.*

She laughs her ghastly laugh and flashes her smile that makes me clench my jaw. *You won't ever be ready*, she giggles, and floats back to my bedroom.

#

I hate the ghost that haunts my house. We take turns threatening each other: I beg her to go and she threatens to leave. We both know I'll back down. I can't let her go.

Instead, I comb my fingers through her milky hair on Thursday nights and ask her how she died. She just looks at me with her lonely empty eyes, and I realize I don't really want to know.

We Were Bred for This

You tell me that the necks warp over time. They swell up and twist, as any wood does, when the humidity changes.

I think of my hair and how it curls in the summer. How limp it is in the winter. How water can make us look different. How much I've changed since I met you.

I try to focus on what you're saying.

You are running your hand along the guitar, showing me places the neck is crooked. "There's a truss rod inside the necks of newer guitars. It helps keep the structure over time." You're talking but I'm not really listening. I'm watching the way your fingers trace along the strings, smooth and sure. The way your eyes look down the length of the guitar, finding flaws I can't see.

"It looks straight to me," I tell you.

"Look closer," you say.

\#

The Dairy Queen is across the street from the slaughterhouse, and we sit on the circular plastic table near the parking lot. I want your feet to bump into mine, but they're tucked underneath you.

We could always tell when it was a slaughter day. The air smells thick and tinny, like dirt and rot. It clings to clothes, to the interior of cars. I fan my sundress around my legs, stirring the air and bringing a waft of decay to my nose. We are used to the smell.

"Do you think they know?" I ask you. You are eating a vanilla cone. It's August in southern Ohio, and your cone is melting faster than you can lick.

I want to take one of your sticky fingers into my mouth and taste the vanilla.

"The pigs? I don't know, maybe. They were bred for this."

It is getting dark and the cicadas' screams are slowing to a rattle. The night creatures would start their chorus soon, filling our silences.

\#

You always use scented plug ins, so your apartment smells like pine.

It's a tiny apartment, but you are so meticulous it feels larger. The sink is clean and your bed is always made.

"Do you even live here?" I ask you, looking at the neatly stacked books on the bedside table.

You don't laugh. "Of course I do. I just like my things where they belong. Each thing in the proper place."

"I try to be clean," I say.

You pull me into a hug. "I like you clean or dirty. I just like you."

Something inside me uncurls, melting under my skin.

\#

We live in farmlands but don't know any farmers. Our town is flat and long, pocketed with warehouses and chain food restaurants. It is all changing: stretches of cornfields churned up and turned into modular homes with a man-made lake in the center, an outlet mall replacing the burned out Chevy factory.

The newness should be ugly, but it isn't. Our town feels alive, a pulse throbbing below its shell.

"We shouldn't come here on slaughter days," I say. "It feels wrong."

"Maybe not. But where else would we go?"

You hand me a napkin so I can clean my hands.

\#

I stay over so often now the apartment feels a bit mine, though you've never asked me to share it. I keep a spare toothbrush in your cabinet, some underwear in your drawer. I only leave the pretty kind — black lace, polka dots.

I tuck these bits of me away into corners and behind closet doors.

You pick up my wine glass before I've had the last sip, wiping down the coaster and table underneath it. You make the bed before I've finished brushing my teeth.

"I'm trying," I tell you.

"I know," you say.

#

We walk along 2nd Street, one of the few older streets in town. There are large retro lightbulbs hung in strings along the street.

I can still smell the slaughterhouse, but it's fainter now. Just a hint amongst the smell of heat and my own sweat.

I want you to stop me under the lights. I want you to hold my face in your hands and lean in and kiss me. I want it to be sweet and taste like ice cream and a hard day.

But you take my hand and pull it towards your mouth, and that is enough for me.

\#

You keep your Christmas lights up all year. You tell me colorful lights shouldn't be seasonal, and I don't disagree. You turn them on after dinner, and they light up your living room in a dim hazy glow.

You take out your guitar and I marvel at your arms as you sling the strap over your back. You have tattoos you don't talk about, and they stand out stark against the wood of the guitar.

Your fingers move fluidly and you close your eyes to sing. I don't sing along; I don't want to ruin your song.

The guitar glitters in the lights and your cheeks are red and blue. You look flushed and I want to trace the circles of color along your cheeks.

After the fifth song I reach forward and take your hand as you finger the strings. We grip the neck of the guitar together as I pull you towards my chest.

\#

You walk me to my apartment door. It's only a few blocks away from yours, and I wish you'd asked me over. You kiss me goodnight and turn to go, but I don't want to say goodbye.

I ask you to wait with me, just wait, because I'm not ready to go inside.

My air conditioning is too strong and it's too bright, too quiet inside on my own.

You put your arm around my shoulder and we lean against the brick of my building. My street is plain: a few townhouses, a few cars parked on the road. There is evidence of people everywhere, but we are alone.

We look up at the stars together, and I search for something to say to make this moment feel right, important. I want to ignore this twist inside of me, this spiral of doubt that threatens to uncurl.

"You're woven into me, you know," I say. It sounds false in my own ears.

You give me a strained smile and pull me closer. I take in the weight of your arm, the feel of your fingertips across my shoulders, the rusty rich smell of slaughter that still haunts us. When you turn to go, I wonder the same thing I always do when you leave me: was this already over? Would I even know if it was?

Home

You say you'd follow him anywhere, so when he asks you to move across the country, you do. You say you'd do anything for love, and you love him.

He wants you to love your life with him.

You try.

Your rented house has plain beige walls. It's in a suburb and has a fenced-in yard. You don't have dogs or children to use it.

The kitchen is tiny. You bump into each other every night as you fix your lunches for the next day. You're watching infants at a childcare center. You change diapers and clean spills all day. You hate it, but there aren't any teaching jobs in October.

You say you'll keep looking for another job. He has his new dream job, after all. A career. He's managing a plant, staying late, getting tipsy at corporate dinners. He comes home rosy cheeked and full of stories about men with names like Bill and Frank. You are never invited.

The point is he's happy. You tell him you'll keep trying.

He's heard you tossing at night, seen you staring at the beige walls, watched you bite the inside of your cheek until your mouth fills with the taste of rust.

He asks you over and over what he can do.

You tell him you miss the sound of the ocean, and the feel of salt air through a cracked window. How the ceiling fan would press the air down and make you feel heavy when you were falling asleep.

He buys a machine that plays the sound of crashing waves and plugs in a fan next to your bed.

You tell him you miss how sand piled in the corners of the kitchen. You miss how the wind carried bits of shell and coral, and how you'd find flecks of it stuck to your scalp when you showered. You miss how you could scratch and scratch all day and still find bits of grit under your nails.

You find a bag of potting sand in the hall closet and perfectly-formed piles near the fridge. One night you wake to him sprinkling sand in your hair; it pools on your pillow and sticks to the sheets. It makes your skin itch.

You tell him it's the air and the smell and the way people dress. You tell him it's the way you could close your eyes and feel present, alive, like a current connected you to the walls of the house. You miss belonging.

He brings in jars of sea air and wears flip flops around the house. He wears Bermuda shorts and Hawaiian shirts to the grocery store. He looks like a parody of your old life together.

What more could you want, he asks you. What else can he do?

You tell him you don't want anything else. There's nothing else he can do.

You can't replicate the heartbeat of a town, or the rhythm of a household, or the texture of a life. Even if you went back now, it would all be different.

So you listen to your sound machine and step over the piles of sand. You tell him it's time to start a new life.

At night, you run your fingers along your scalp and look under your nails for traces of sand.

Beautiful, Violent Things

I will always remember that it was dusk because of what you always tell me (*always told me*)—that I am attracted to beautiful, violent things. You were right of course; I love dusk and dusk is the most violent of times. Lines are blurred and shapes deceive you and you think something is there and it really isn't (*the huddled figure in the cornfield is just a fence's shadow, not a man squatting in the fields*) and the deer are reckless at dusk, sprinting into the road searching for food, not knowing or caring that the time changed and that you need to get home so I don't notice that you're late (*I stopped looking at the clock a long time ago*). You were probably thinking about how dusk always seems heavy as it's falling, like a thick blanket of fog over the farms, coating the hills in gray before pitching into endless black (*violent, violent*). You were probably wondering if I was home yet, if I was making you dinner (*I wasn't*). You were maybe wondering if I was planning something for your birthday, if I noticed you were going gray, if I'd smell the guilt on you like hot liquor breath (*I wasn't, I didn't, I probably wouldn't have*). Did you think of me when the doe stepped a spindly leg into the road, slowly, head turning to look into your headlights? Did you remember how I warned you to look along the edges of the woods at dusk to scan for the glint of eyes? Did you think of me as your car collided with the doe, throwing you forward and the doe backward, both bodies hitting the road with a thud? Did you know the doe survived? As your blood left your body and soaked into the summer-scorched pavement, as your vision started to blur as you watched the doe stand up and hobble away, did you wonder if I was missing you? (*I wasn't*).

Acknowledgments

These stories were originally published in the following publications:

Tell Me I'm Different - *Cleaver Magazine*

Punk Rock Princess - *Memoir Mixtapes*

When Your Ex-Lover Walks on the Moon - *Cease, Cows*

Mary, Wendy, Rosalita - *Shut Down Strangers and Hot Rod Angels*

Call if You Don't Feel Better in Two Weeks - *Little Fiction, Big Truths*

What We Bury - *Barren Magazine*

The Ghost that Haunts my House - *New Flash Fiction Review*

We Were Bred for This - *Breadcrumbs Magazine* (originally published as "Breadcrumb #389")

Home - *X-R-A-Y Literary Magazine*

Beautiful, Violent Things - *matchbook*